Teggs is no ordinary dinosaur –
he's an **ASTROSAUR!** Captain of
the amazing spaceship DSS *Sauropod*,
he goes on dange
fights evil – along
crew, Gipsy, A

For more astro-fun visit the website
www.astrosaurs.co.uk

Find out more at www.astrosaurs.co.uk

# Astrosaurs

## THE FOREST OF EVIL

Steve Cole

*Illustrated by* Woody Fox

**RED FOX**

**THE FOREST OF EVIL**
**A RED FOX BOOK 978 1 849 41395 4**

First published in Great Britain by Red Fox,
an imprint of Random House Children's Books
A Random House Group Company

This edition published 2011

1 3 5 7 9 10 8 6 4 2

Text copyright © Steve Cole, 2011
Cover illustration and cards © Dynamo Design, 2011
Map visual © Charlie Fowkes, 2005
Illustrations by Woody Fox, © Random House Children's Books, 2011

The Random House Group Limited supports the Forest Stewardship
Council ® (FSC ®), the leading international forest certification organization.
All our titles that are printed on Greenpeace-approved FSC ®-certified paper
carry the FSC ® logo. Our paper procurement policy can be found at
www.randomhouse.co.uk/environment.

MIX
Paper from
responsible sources
FSC® C016897

Typeset in Bembo MT Schoolbook 16/20pt
by Falcon Oast Graphic Art Ltd.

Red Fox Books are published by Random House Children's Books,
61–63 Uxbridge Road, London W5 5SA

Address es for c         thin The Random House Group L mited can

TH                                              UP Limited Reg. No. 9       009

A CIP c                                                        m the Brit   h Library.

Printed an      nd in Great Britain b   CPI Bookmarque, Croyd n   , CR0 4TD

*For Zakaria Meddour*

# WARNING!

## THINK YOU KNOW ABOUT DINOSAURS?

### THINK AGAIN!

The dinosaurs . . .
  Big, stupid, lumbering reptiles. Right?
  All they did was eat, sleep and roar a bit. Right?
  Died out millions of years ago when a big meteor struck the Earth. Right?

*Wrong!*

The dinosaurs weren't stupid. They may have had small brains, but they used them well. They had big thoughts and big dreams.

By the time the meteor hit, the last dinosaurs had already left Earth for ever. Some breeds had discovered how to travel through space as early as the Triassic period, and were already enjoying a new life among the stars. No one has found evidence of dinosaur technology yet. But the first fossil bones were only unearthed in 1822, and new finds are being made all the time.

The proof is out there, buried in the ground.

And the dinosaurs live on, way out in space, even now. They've settled down in a place they call the Jurassic Quadrant and over the last sixty-five million years they've gone on evolving.

The dinosaurs we'll be meeting are

 part of a special group called the Dinosaur Space Service. Their job is to explore space, to go on exciting missions and to fight evil and protect the innocent!

These heroic herbivores are not just dinosaurs.

They are *astrosaurs*!

NOTE: *The following story has been translated from secret Dinosaur Space Service records. Earthling dinosaur names are used throughout, although some changes have been made for easy reading. There's even a guide to help you pronounce the dinosaur names on the next page.*

# Talking Dinosaur!

How to say the prehistoric
names in this book . . .

STEGOSAURUS –
*STEG-oh-SORE-us*

IGUANODON –
*ig-WHA-noh-don*

TRICERATOPS –
*try-SERRA-tops*

HADROSAUR –
*HAD-roh-SORE*

GIGANTOSAURUS –
*jy-GANT-uh-SORE-us*

DIMORPHODON
*– die-MORF-oh-don*

LAMBEOSAUR –
*LAM-be-oh-SORE*

# THE CREW OF THE DSS SAUROPOD

**CAPTAIN
TEGGS STEGOSAUR**

**ARX ORANO,**
FIRST OFFICER

**GIPSY SAURINE,**
COMMUNICATIONS
OFFICER

**IGGY TOOTH,**
CHIEF ENGINEER

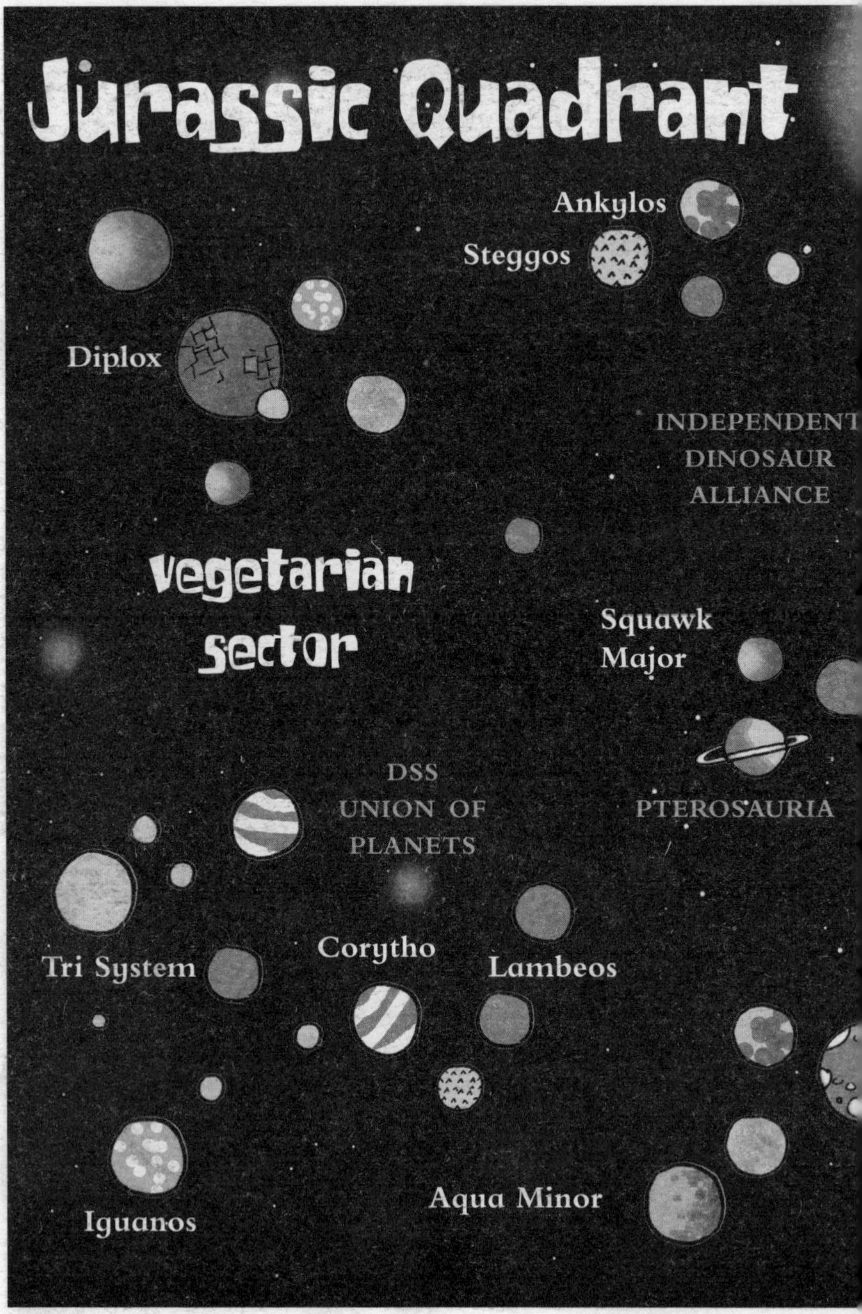

# Jurassic Quadrant

Ankylos

Steggos

Diplox

INDEPENDENT
DINOSAUR
ALLIANCE

## vegetarian

## sector

Squawk
Major

DSS
UNION OF
PLANETS

PTEROSAURIA

Tri System

Corytho

Lambeos

Iguanos

Aqua Minor

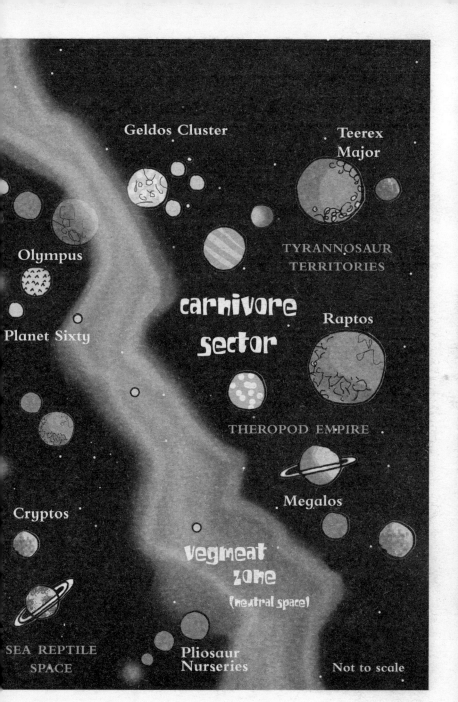

# THE
# FOREST OF
# EVIL

## Chapter One

## THE POISONED PLANET

"Great galaxies!" Captain Teggs Stegosaur stared through the windows of his shuttlecraft in dismay. "I've never seen such a poorly looking planet." He turned to his crewmates. "Have you?"

Arx the triceratops, Iggy the iguanodon and Gipsy the hadrosaur all shook their heads in stunned amazement. As top-class astrosaurs – the pride of the Dinosaur Space Service – they had explored hundreds of incredible worlds in their

1

spaceship, the *Sauropod*.

But never one like this.

Noxia-4 was a farm-planet, and to Teggs that brought to mind green meadows rich with mouthwatering plants. But all he could see were wilted leaves and dusty stalks, stretching out in every direction.

"It's like a dustbowl," Teggs remarked as the shuttle came in to land. "I thought there were meant to be endless rolling fields?"

"It looks like they rolled over and died!" said Iggy, the *Sauropod*'s rough and tough mechanic.

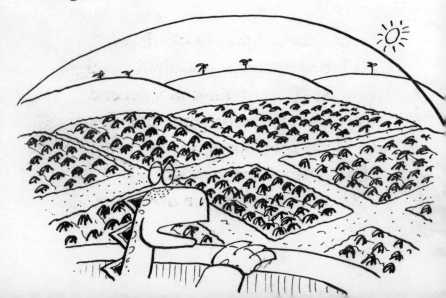

"No wonder the planet's farmers sent that mysterious message for help," said Arx, Teggs's bright green First Officer. "Remember what they said?"

"Strange things happening, please send astrosaurs, wibble-wibble," recalled Gipsy, who was in charge of communications. "Funny sort of distress signal – especially as they sent it to a greengrocer's on the planet Steggos instead of to us!"

Arx nodded. "It took three whole days for the message to reach DSS HQ, and another day for us to get here. In all that time, no other messages were sent – and the farmers haven't answered any of our calls."

Teggs opened the shuttle doors. "We'd better start investigating straight away. Millions of dinosaurs depend on food from farm-planets like this one. If the problems spread to the nine neighbouring crop-worlds . . ."

"There will be famine across the

3

Vegetarian Sector," Arx concluded.

"According to our maps, the dino-farmers' dwelling dome should be just over this hill." Teggs led the way outside. "Let's check it out."

The astrosaurs trudged away through dry mud and dead plants. Farm machines — turbo-tractors, robo-reapers and sprinkler-bots — stood scattered around, abandoned. The only sounds were the crump of their footsteps and the wind rustling withered leaves.

"There it is," said Gipsy as they reached the top of the hill. "The dwelling dome!"

The dome was like the cap of some giant metal mushroom growing out of the soil — an all-in-one living space for the farmers who worked here. It stood at the end of a wide path leading down the sloping hillside. But in all other directions, the dome was surrounded by a vast, sprawling forest of twisted, spindly trees and thick, thorny bushes.

Iggy licked his lips. "That forest looks good enough to eat."

"It *is*," Arx agreed. "That's why it's on the dome's doorstep. The crops are needed on other worlds, so the farmers feed on the forest – that's the way it works on all farm planets."

"Well, I could nosh a leaf or two myself," said Teggs, his tum rumbling as always. "Let's have

a quick bite, just to keep us going while
we explore ..."

He led his friends down the slope
towards the forest's edge and was just
about to chomp on some juicy-looking
branches when—

*ZZZAP!*

A laser blast scorched over his head
and a tree went up in smoke.

"Don't move!" came a
hoarse cry from outside
the dome.

Teggs, Gipsy, Arx
and Iggy looked over
to find a wild-eyed
lambeosaur in muddy
dungarees and a wide
straw hat, holding a
laser rifle.

"It's all right," Teggs
called. "We're peaceful
astrosaurs. We've come
to help you."

"I'm glad about that." The dinosaur kept a tight grip on his gun. "My name's Leefer. I *had* to shoot – to warn you away from that forest."

Gipsy frowned. "But why?"

"Because if you go in there, you'll disappear like all the others," Leefer warned them. "Mark my words, astrosaurs – that's a forest of evil. Those who step inside are never seen again!"

Once Teggs had introduced himself and his crew, Leefer invited them inside the dome. "Sorry about the mess," the farmer said. "I wasn't expecting company."

The farmers' dome looked like a giant indoor field – one that had been trampled by runaway mammoths. Six straw beds lay scattered around the circular edge of the dome, but only one looked slept in. The ceiling was tiled with TV screens showing views of different dusty fields across the planet, and in the middle was a large living space with tatty sofas and chairs. The floor was made of muddy grass. Teggs had a nibble but it tasted of farmers' feet. "Yuk!"

"I'm sure glad you're here," said Leefer. "I've been real lonely."

As he closed the dome's door, Gipsy noticed a strong, sickly sweet smell. "Ugh!" She held her nose. "What's that stink?"

"I hope you're not talking about my aftershave," said Leefer sharply.

Teggs took a cautious sniff – then gasped. "She is!"

"I mixed it myself." Leefer looked put out. "It's better then smelling of muck and sweat like all the other farmers. 'Sweet-pong Leefer', they call me."

"They should call you *Lucky* Leefer, if you're the only farmer left," noted Arx. "Was it you who sent the call for help?"

"Nope. That was Chief Farmer Frisbee," said Leefer. "He sent it just before he went completely doo-lally."

"Doo-lally?" Teggs echoed. "Do you mean he wasn't well?"

"He started saying and doing crazy things," Leefer explained. "As soon as he sent that call for help, he smashed up the communicator. See? Crazy!"

Gipsy eyed the broken equipment. "So that's why you didn't reply to our calls."

"The last two weeks have been terrible." Leefer shrugged sadly. "First the crops started to die. Then Frisbee went crazy. And not long after, the other farmers went crazy too, one after the other, and ran off into the forest."

Iggy counted the beds again. "Were there really only six of you farming the whole planet?"

"Sure. Robots do all the tough stuff," Leefer explained. "They plough the fields, sow the seeds, harvest the crops – and we oversee things from here in the dome." He pointed to the screens on the ceiling. "Clever cameras give us a perfect

view of every last field on the planet. My main job is looking after them. 'Camera-Expert Leefer' they call me."

Teggs nodded. "Did your cameras show anything strange or suspicious two weeks ago – around the time the plants started dying?"

"It was just after a real bad thunderstorm, so it was dark and cloudy," Leefer recalled. "But I didn't see nothing."

"I'd like to study these poisoned crops to see what's wrong with them," said Arx. "Do you have any samples?"

"Nope. And I can't get none, neither," said Leefer. "See, Chief Farmer Frisbee thought the crops had been poisoned on purpose by someone – or something – from space. So he made Yokul programme the robots to protect them – or what's left of them – at all costs."

"Who's Yokul?" asked Teggs.

"Our robot expert," said Leefer. "'Robot-Expert Yokul', we called him."

"Well, can't you just turn the robots off?" asked Gipsy.

Leefer shook his head. "Only Yokul can do that. And he was the second of us farmers to go fruit-loops and vanish into the forest."

Arx waggled his horns thoughtfully. "It's quite unusual for a robot expert to go into farming, isn't it?"

"Oh, Yokul just loved nature and wildlife. It was his hobby, you know?" Leefer sighed. "Three days ago, we all went deep into the forest looking for Frisbee. We didn't have no luck, but Yokul said he'd found something incredible out there . . . Something terrible and scary . . ."

Gipsy gulped. "What?"

"Dunno. Yokul went batty as a bathtub before he could tell us! He ran around bopping himself on the head, then rushed out into the forest. He never came back. I was so sad." He sniffed. "'So-Sad Leefer', they called me."

"Didn't you go after him?" asked Arx.

"Course! The rest of us looked all over that darned forest." Leefer shook his head. "Not a trace of either of them. And then the other three went loopy too. It's that forest, I tell you! It used to be fine . . . but now it's turned evil!"

"Well, dinosaurs don't just disappear," said Teggs. "And forests are food, not frightening. I think it's time we found your friends – and solved this mystery." He jumped up. "Robots or no robots, we need some crop samples for

Arx to study. Iggy, you're a top mechanic – see if you can undo whatever Yokul did."

Iggy rolled up his sleeves. "I'll get un-programming right away!"

Teggs smiled. "Arx, Gipsy – you come with me. It's time we explored these wild woods."

Arx saluted, and Gipsy swallowed hard. "Let's just hope that whatever happened to the farmers doesn't happen to us!"

## Chapter Two

## INTO THE FOREST

Teggs strode from the
dome and paused at the
edge of the forbidding
forest. The thick, twisted
trees stood tall as
houses, their branches
tangling high
overhead, blocking out
the sunlight. Strange,
alien plants stood
about like sentries.

Leefer followed Teggs
out with Gipsy and Arx. "Er . . . I don't
have to come with you, do I? After losing
so many of my friends in there . . ."

"Why not stay and help Iggy?" Teggs suggested.

Gipsy surveyed the forest. "It is a bit spooky, isn't it? Especially with creepy plants like *that* around." She pointed to a huge spindly thing standing some way inside the forest.

Teggs frowned. It looked like an overgrown Venus fly-trap. It had thick roots and its stem was crowned with a bulging, bell-shaped bud almost like a head. A big, blue butterfly fluttered past – and the bud split open like a hungry mouth. *SNAP!* The plant's jaws snapped shut and the butterfly was no more.

"Ugh," said Gipsy. "That poor little insect."

"A whole lot of bugs

get eaten by them there plants," Leefer explained. "That's why Yokul named 'em 'fearblooms'. He just loved studying them 'cause they're real mysterious. They've never been found nowhere else." Leefer kicked a twig, sadly. "I sure hope you find him, and the others."

"So do I," said Teggs. "Ask Iggy to call us once you've got the crop sample – and we'll call him if we find trouble!"

"Will do," said Leefer gratefully, scurrying back inside.

Quietly, carefully, Teggs ventured into the silent forest.

Arx and Gipsy stayed close behind, and all three kept well away from the fearbloom.

The deeper they went, the gloomier the woods became.

"Look!" Gipsy pointed with delight as another beautiful blue butterfly flew past. "I'm glad those horrid fearblooms haven't scoffed them all." The butterfly settled lightly on her head for a moment as if to thank her. Then it fluttered away.

Teggs followed its progress – and as it passed a large tree, he frowned.

"Hey, look. That bark's been badly scratched."

Arx and Gipsy studied the gashes in the trunk.

"They look like claw marks to me," said Gipsy.

"And look *here*." Arx nudged the muddy forest floor with his nose. "Footprints!"

Teggs inspected the tracks. "They're enormous."

"Whoever left them should be easy to find," said Gipsy nervously. "It looks like they were heading into the middle of the forest."

"Let's follow them," said Teggs.

Slowly and quietly, the three astrosaurs moved deeper into the wild wood . . .

"Blast this computer!" Iggy cried crossly. Working in the dome's control centre with Leefer, he was tangled up in wires. "Blast it to bits!"

Leefer raised his laser rifle. "OK, if you insist."

"No!" said Iggy quickly. "I'm only saying 'Blast it' because I'm cross. The computer won't let me switch off the robots – Yokul programmed it too well."

"I've always hated computers," Leefer grumbled. "'Computer-hating Leefer', they call me."

"Well, we need those crop samples," said Iggy, crossing to the door. "So we'll just have to take some."

Leefer splashed on some more pongy aftershave, then followed Iggy out into the sunshine to the field at the top of the hill.

"There! Plenty of withered plants going begging." Iggy crouched to pull one out from the soil. "If I'm quick, those

robots won't even notice – YEEOW!"
Suddenly, he found himself sprayed with
a high-speed stream of seeds. The tiny
missiles stung his skin, stuck in his eyes
and got in his nose and mouth. "Urph!"
Iggy spluttered, jumping backwards.
The seed spray only stopped once he
was clear of the field. Iggy wiped his
watering eyes and saw a small red,
cannon-shaped robot further along the
field, pointed his way. "What is that
thing?"

"An automatic seed-sower," said Leefer
ruefully. "That was just a warning. I
saw Yokul test them – if you try to steal
another plant, it'll hit you harder."

Iggy scowled. "With more seeds, I
suppose?"

"Yep." Leefer helped him up. "Only this
time it'll fire them when they're still in
their packets."

"Then I'll use a shield," Iggy declared.
He ran down the hill, used his thumb

spikes to tear off some tree bark, and held it up like a riot shield. "This'll fix it."

"I don't think so," said Leefer.

As soon as Iggy set foot on the field, the automatic sower fired seed packets at a hundred miles per hour. They bounced harmlessly off his tree-bark shield. "Ha!" said Iggy, and crouched to grab another plant . . .

This time, a turbo-tractor came zooming up – and ran Iggy over! "OOOF!" he gasped as its huge wheels squashed him flat into the mud. As he struggled up, a sprinkler-bot squirted water in his face, fifty times faster

than a firefighter's
hose.

Coughing and
gasping in the
flood of water,
Iggy was again
forced back off
the field where he
collapsed in a squashed, soggy heap.

"Told you so," said Leefer glumly.

"I'm not beaten," Iggy growled. "We'll
get that crop sample
yet – just you wait
and see!"

Deep in the dark
forest, Teggs, Arx
and Gipsy were
facing struggles of
their own. "We've
lost the trail of
whatever made those
footprints," Teggs grumbled.

"Oh well." Gipsy nudged him in the ribs. "We did say we wanted to explore!"

They pressed on. The vegetation grew thicker and thornier. Teggs started walking backwards, swinging his spiky tail from side to side to clear a path for his friends.

"Wait!" Arx held up a paw in warning. "I think I heard something."

Teggs listened hard. Sure enough, in the distance, he could hear something crashing through the undergrowth. "It's getting louder."

Arx nodded gravely. "We might have lost that unknown creature's trail . . . but now I think it's *found* ours!"

## Chapter Three

## BLOOMING AWFUL!

Teggs tensed himself for action, as the clattering, crashing noise grew ever louder.

Suddenly, an enormous dinosaur exploded through the branches and brambles! It reared up and its jaws swung open, revealing rows of super-sharp teeth. Grey fabric hung in tatters from its powerful body, and its short, stocky arms ended in vicious claws.

Arx gasped. Gipsy's headcrest flushed blue with alarm, and Teggs prepared to fight . . .

But then he realized the carnivore wasn't even looking at them. It had gone cross-eyed, and was waggling its tongue to make funny bibbling noises. "Wibble!" it cried, and then hit itself on the head with its tail – *BOMP!* – and laughed.

"What's it doing?" hissed Gipsy.

"I have no idea," Teggs admitted.

"We scientists have a name for this sort of behaviour," said Arx. "We call it 'going completely nutty-bonkers'!"

The fearsome dinosaur whacked itself on the head again. Then it

giggled and ran past them, tearing its
way through the thick forest until it was
lost from sight.

"Where did that thing come from?"
said Gipsy shakily. "It looked like a
T-rex."

"Close," said Arx. "I think it was a
gigantosaurus."

"At least now we know what made
those tracks," said Teggs grimly.
"Gigantosaurus are smarter than T-rexes,
and a whole lot sneakier."

"But what is that one doing here?"
Gipsy wondered.

"Let's find out!" Teggs pelted
off in pursuit of the runaway
gigantosaurus, his friends
close behind him. The
carnivore had torn a ragged
pathway through the
undergrowth that
made it easy to
follow.

"That
thing said
'wibble'," Arx panted as they ran. "I just
remembered – Frisbee said 'wibble' too,
in his distress call."

Teggs nodded. "Perhaps he discovered
that gigantosaurus but it turned him
funny to stop him warning anyone
properly."

"And then he chased it into the forest." Gipsy ducked to avoid a broken tree branch. "Never to be seen again . . ."

Suddenly a terrible yowl of pain cut through the forest, quickly followed by the sounds of a violent struggle.

"Sounds like our meat-munching mate," said Teggs, galloping even faster. "Come on!"

The three astrosaurs burst from the trees like bullets into a gloomy glade. But what they saw there froze them, speechless, in their tracks.

The gigantosaurus had fallen into a clump of fearblooms – and the fleshy plants were biting and chomping it all

over! Caught
in the thick
tentacles
of the
fearblooms'
roots, the
carnivore
couldn't break
free as the plants
dragged it down into the mud.

Teggs wanted to help the carnivore
– but knew it was already too late. In
a matter of seconds, the dinosaur was
completely buried and the fearblooms
wriggled down into the mud after it.
Then a sinister silence returned to the
forest.

Gipsy held her stomach. "I feel sick."

"It seems fearblooms were named with
good reason," said Teggs grimly.
"I wonder who that gigantosaurus
was?"

"This should tell us." Arx stooped to

30

pick up a grey scrap of material with a plastic disk inside. "It's an ID card – the dino must have lost this in its struggle to get free."

Teggs read the scrawled writing. "Captain Krokk, Carnivore Space Force, Sneaky Missions Squad."

"How did he get here?" Arx wondered. "And if his mission was sneaky, why was he drawing attention to himself?"

"Do you think Krokk is the one who's killed all the crops?" Gipsy shivered. "And are there others here like him?"

"That's what we've got to find out." Teggs pulled out his communicator. "I think it's time we called in some help . . ."

Back in the fields beyond the forest, Iggy was still trying to pinch plant samples – and getting crosser, muckier and more and more sore with every failed attempt.

He'd made a fishing rod and tried to hook out some withered leaves. But a robo-reaper sliced his stick in half.

He'd tried to sneak up on the failed crops wearing a gorse bush as a disguise. But another turbo-tractor rolled along and ran him over.

"I told you it couldn't be done," said Leefer sadly. "'Know-it-all Leefer', they call me."

Iggy glared at him – and then his communicator bleeped. "Iggy here. Captain, is that you?"

"It certainly is," came Teggs's voice. "Get to the shuttle, Ig. Call the *Sauropod* and tell the dimorphodon to get down here straight away."

Leefer frowned. "Who are the dimorphodon?"

"Our flight crew," Iggy explained. "Fifty flying reptiles who help steer the spaceship." He spoke back into the communicator: "That's a great idea, Captain! See, the robots won't let me take any crop samples, but I bet Sprite and his flying mates could whizz around and catch the robots out!"

"Nice idea, Ig, but I'm afraid Leefer will have to try and get that sample by himself," said Teggs. "First of all, I need the dimorphodon to search this forest from above – and I need *you* to help us look around at ground level. We've found something nasty – and there may be others like it!"

Iggy jumped up. "I'll get to the shuttle

right away. Over and out."

"I'd like to know what's he found," said Leefer worriedly. "And I'd also like to know how he expects *me* to get a crop sample if you couldn't? Does he think I can magic one from out of the ground?"

A slow grin spread over Iggy's face. "Perhaps you can magic one from *under* the ground! Are you any good at digging?"

"Give me a super-spade and watch me go!" said Leefer proudly. "'Big-digger Leefer', they call me."

"Then get digging, big-digger." Iggy slapped him on the back. "Make a tunnel in the hillside just under the field – and pull the crops down by the *roots*. The robots will never notice!"

"That's a clever plan." Leefer smiled. "You leave it to me."

"I'm afraid I'll have to," said Iggy, running off to the shuttle. "Good luck, and don't let the robots bring you down – at least, not until you've brought down one of those plants!"

Back in the forest, Gipsy was poking the muddy ground that had swallowed Captain Krokk. It looked like a freshly dug flower bed, the soil newly turned in big crumbly clods.

Teggs lowered his communicator and he and Arx came to join her. "It's hard to believe anything ever happened here."

Gipsy nodded. "How could the fearblooms wriggle underground like that? Do you think they've . . . eaten him?"

"So it seems." Arx shrugged. "Dinosaurs have been eating plants for millions of

35

years. Now it seems we've found one that bites back!"

"Well, carnivores bite harder," Teggs reminded his friends. "So we'd better start searching for others. Iggy is calling the dimorphodon to help us. In the meantime, Arx, you search south, I'll head east, and Gipsy, you go west."

"Yes, Captain," chorused Arx and Gipsy.

Gipsy rubbed her tummy as she walked away into the thick forest. She really wasn't feeling well. "But I can't rest now," she muttered. "We've got a job to do – and astrosaurs never give up."

On and on she went, over a stream, past fallen tree trunks, forcing her way through the thick forest. Finally she paused for breath in a small clearing.

*SNAP!*

Gipsy froze. It sounded like a twig snapping underfoot. Could someone be

36

trying to sneak up behind her?

Then a cloud of big blue butterflies fluttered into the clearing. Gipsy let out a huge sigh of relief, and the beautiful insects flew happily around her. One landed on her hoof, another tickled her nose. Laughing, she gently blew it away . . .

Just as four fearblooms poked their ugly heads out of the close-by

undergrowth – and somehow started
to *move*. Gipsy stared in horror as
the towering plants used their thick,
twitching roots like legs.

Jaws swinging open, they rushed
towards her . . .

## Chapter Four

## FOREST TRICKERY

"The lady's not for chomping," growled Gipsy. She jumped into a dino-judo fighting stance, scattering butterflies in all directions, ready to drive off her weird attackers ...

But then a shower of purple liquid sprayed out from the forest behind her and coated the closest fearbloom. *SMOOSH!* It shrivelled up, its stalk blackening, leaves withering away.

The other fearblooms snapped their jaws and rattled their roots – then turned and retreated back into the greenery.

Gipsy turned to thank her rescuer. "Thank space you came when you . . . did?"

Her words trailed off as another

grey gigantosaurus stepped into the clearing. Massive and muscular, it wore a black skullcap. Jars full of powders and potions clinked together in a belt around its middle. Its yellow eyes shone cold and cunning, and Gipsy almost choked on the sharp whiff of chemicals that came off the creature.

She raised her hooves in warning.

"Who are you?"

"My name is Gucklock," the sinister figure replied.

"Well, I've got some bad news for you, Gucklock. Your captain's been got by the fearblooms."

"I was afraid of that," he said quietly. "How inconvenient."

"You carnivores are completely cold-hearted, aren't you?" Gipsy scowled. "But since you've lost your leader – you may as well give up now."

"No, little plant-eater," growled Gucklock. "*You* will surrender to me – for I have need of you and your astrosaur friends ..." He opened a glass tube and threw yellow powder at Gipsy. With a choking gasp, she felt cold all over – and then she felt nothing at all ...

★ Half an
hour later
and two
miles away,
Teggs was
climbing through
clumps of blue bracken, every sense
alert for trouble. Now Iggy and the
dimorphodon had joined in the search
to the north, they were covering ground
quickly. Led by chief dino-bird Sprite,
the flying reptiles flitted from branch to
branch, keen eyes scanning the forest for
anything unusual.

All Teggs had spotted so far were a
couple of lurking fearblooms, biting at
butterflies. Teggs threw a big stick at the
plants and they snapped at it crossly.
One butterfly settled briefly on his arm
before taking off again.

Suddenly, Teggs heard a crackling noise
to his right. His back-plates flushed red

and he raised his tail to strike.

But it was only Iggy, scrambling through dead leaves to join him. "Found anything, Captain?"

Teggs shook his head. "Only you, Ig!" Then a flying reptile clattered down from some high branches to land on Iggy's cap. "And here's Sprite. Anything to report?"

Sprite let out a series of clicks and whistles and shook his head crossly.

"That'll be a no, then," said Iggy.

Teggs's communicator beeped. "Arx here, sir," came the triceratops's familiar voice. "Nothing to report so far."

"That just leaves Gipsy. She hasn't called in yet." Teggs pressed a button on his communicator. "Hello, Gipsy? Are you there?"

A hoot of dismay sounded in the distance.

Iggy jumped, sending his cap – and Sprite – flying. "She's *there*, Captain. I'd know her hoots anywhere."

Teggs nodded, staring around wildly. "It sounds like she's in trouble."

"Eeep!" cried Sprite, flapping up and sniffing the air. "Chrrrp!"

"He's got her scent!" Teggs cried, as Sprite flapped away. "Iggy, he can lead us straight to her!"

The two friends charged off after Sprite, crashing through bushes, storming through swamps and barging through brambles. Teggs barely felt the sting of thorns or the bruises of branches.

He just kept on following Sprite as the plucky dino-bird dived this way and that through the forest's dense design.

The trees grew more and more twisted and more and more tangled. Giant bushes towered all around, their black leaves caked in yellow mould. Brambles grew in odd, misshapen clumps. There was a sharp chemical tang to the air.

*Something nasty's happened here,* thought Teggs.

Sprite flapped up to perch in a treetop to get a better view, when suddenly – *CLANNNG!* He bounced straight off the branch, dazed senseless! He went into a nosedive but Teggs caught him just in time.

"Urp," said Sprite, rubbing his beak.

"The tree is metal?" Teggs translated. Then he peered carefully at the view in front of him – a massive tree, some red ivy, and pale green sky up above. But somehow it all seemed oddly flat. Almost like an enormous photograph . . .

Iggy pulled an astro-wrench from his belt and tapped the tree. It rang like metal – just as Sprite had said! "This isn't part of the forest, Captain." He started tapping the ivy, which clanged in just the same way. "Our eyes are playing tricks on us. A super-sneaky gadget is *disguising* the true appearance of whatever's here."

"And stopping us from reaching Gipsy." In frustration, Teggs thumped the metal tree with his tail – and with a sparking bang, the view began to shimmer and blur. In a matter of moments, the vision of the tree and the ivy was gone . . .

And Teggs, Sprite and Iggy were left gaping at a gigantic space rocket, taller than the blackened trees all around! A crimson skull was stencilled on the side.

"The mark of meat-eaters," Teggs
breathed – as Gipsy hooted for help
more urgently.

"She must be on the other side of this
ship," Iggy cried.

Teggs tried to squeeze through the overgrown tangle of bushes and trees. "Sprite, you go on ahead."

Sprite zoomed away like a missile, up and over the top of the rocket – and then *his* cry of alarm joined Gipsy's in a great, hooting squawk.

"Faster, Iggy!" In desperation, Teggs started chewing his way through the gnarled wood like a demented beaver, while Iggy slashed away with his thumbspikes. 'We've got to help them before it's too late!'

## Chapter Five

## THE DOORS OF DEATH

Finally, Teggs and Iggy broke through the barricade of trees. They saw Gipsy tied up with plant vines ... Sprite pecking madly at the knots ...

And four fearblooms scuttling towards her on wriggling root–legs!

"Clear off!" Teggs bellowed at the
plants. He jumped through the air and
lashed out his tail. Two of the plants
cringed away, but the other two lunged
forward to bite him.

Iggy threw his cap like a discus and
clobbered one, knocking it back – but its
friend chowed down on Teggs's arm.

Gasping, Teggs tore himself free –
and Sprite pecked the fearbloom like a
woodpecker, right on its roots. Thrashing
and swaying, the plant retreated and the
others scuttled after it into the shadows
of the forest.

"Oh, Captain!" Gipsy cried. "And Iggy, Sprite, I'm so glad to see you. Are you all right?"

Teggs checked the bite mark on his aching arm. The plant's jaw had left a smear of yellow slime and he quickly wiped it on some grass. "I'm fine — I think."

Iggy helped Sprite to untie Gipsy's wrists. "What happened to you?"

"Another gigantosaurus," said Gipsy, pulling her hands free as Teggs worked on the vines around her feet. "A proper charmer called Gucklock. He said he

51

needed me for something and threw some kind of powder at me. The next thing I knew, I was here." She looked behind her and gasped. "Huh? There was no spaceship there a minute ago!"

"There was," Iggy assured her. "But it was in disguise." He pointed to a black box stuck to the rocket's side by a spaghetti of cables. "See that? It's a class-one delusion engine – it made the whole ship look like a part of the forest so no one noticed it."

Teggs untied Gipsy's feet and she wriggled them gratefully. "Ig, now that we *have* noticed it," he said, "what do you think it is?"

Iggy was marvelling at the vessel.

"I reckon it's a Solar-Storm warship."

"I read a DSS spy report on those,"
Teggs recalled. "Solar-Storms are
secret, experimental crafts
created by the Carnivore
Space Force. They don't
run on burning dung
like most spaceships.
They are powered by a
miniature sun."

"A sun?" Gipsy
boggled.

"A small ball of
super-heated mega-fire,"
Iggy explained. "It lets the Solar-
Storm travel close to the speed of light."

"Just the job for sneaky missions."
Gipsy tried to stand, dizzily. "I bet Krokk
and his crew used it to zoom down here
in the blink of an eye."

"And then disguised it so no one would
know they were here," Teggs added. "But
I heard that the Solar-Storms aren't very

safe – those tiny stars are so powerful
they're hard to contain."

Iggy nodded. "Several prototypes
blew themselves to bits – along with the
planets they were parked on!"

Gipsy shuddered. "Let's hope they've
perfected the wibble!"

Teggs frowned. "Pardon?"

"Er, the design, I mean," Gipsy said
quickly.

"You sure you're feeling all right?"
Iggy asked worriedly.

"I feel a bit rotten," Gipsy admitted.
"Ever since that ho-wibble – I mean,
*horrible* – Gucklock threw his powder at
me."

"Eeep-cheep?" Sprite asked suddenly.

"Good question," said Teggs. "I don't
know why this Gucklock tied up Gipsy
and left her outside his ship in plain sight.
But I do know he'll be sorry for it."

Iggy pointed to a wide metal shutter
in the side of the warship.

"He must be hiding in there."
"Well, he won't escape us," said Teggs. "We'll charge the door on the count of three. One . . . two . . . !"

"Three!" Iggy joined in with his captain's cry, lowered his shoulder and ran at the shutter.

*KA-ZZZZZZZ!*

An electric blaze of light engulfed the two astrosaurs. They cried out in pain and strained to pull free – but they were stuck helplessly to the door.

"Captain! Iggy!" Gipsy started forward to help. "What's happening?"

"Keep back!" groaned Teggs, his scaly skin starting to steam.

"It's . . . an . . . anti–intruder device,"

Iggy panted, his skull searing with pain. "Touch us and . . . you'll get fried . . . too!"

"We must do something, Sprite!" Gipsy frowned. "Wibble-wibble . . . I mean, try and reach that wibble – that *control panel* – up there!"

Sprite wasn't sure about Gipsy's wibbles, but his keen eye spotted the controls she was talking about, high above the door. He flapped up, twisted

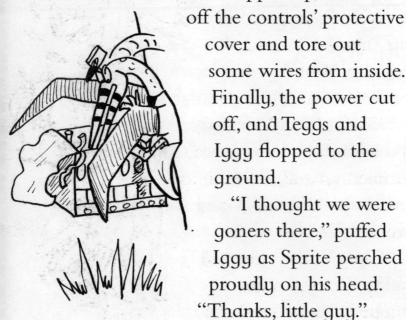

off the controls' protective cover and tore out some wires from inside. Finally, the power cut off, and Teggs and Iggy flopped to the ground.

"I thought we were goners there," puffed Iggy as Sprite perched proudly on his head. "Thanks, little guy."

"And well done for spotting those controls, Gipsy," added Teggs. "They must maintain the power to the ship's defences. But what made you say wibble, like Krokk — and like Frisbee? Are you sure you're OK?"

Just then, Arx rushed into the clearing with a load of dimorphodon on his back and a butterfly balanced on his nose-horn. "I heard the shouts and came running. What's going on?"

"Wibble," replied Gipsy. Then she went cross-eyed, jumped up and ran off into the forest, "wibbling" and wobbling as she went.

"Gipsy!" Teggs shouted as the dimorphodon flapped around in alarm.

"What's wrong with her?" asked Iggy, baffled.

"She's gone the same way as Captain Krokk!" said Arx.

"And possibly Frisbee and the farmers too." Teggs started off into the undergrowth. "Iggy, try to get that door open. Arx, come with me – we've got to bring Gipsy back!"

The two friends ran full pelt through the forest, trampling everything in their path. But as they rounded a bushy corner . . .

"Oh, no!" Teggs yelled. "Gipsy!"

Just like Krokk, Gipsy had been captured by the fearblooms. The big, spindly plants were snapping at her arms and legs, and the soil beneath her churned as they tried to drag her underground.

"No, you don't!" Teggs dived towards the plants, which reared up as he approached like a nest of serpents. He tried to squash them, but they started biting at him too – and they were fiercely strong, tangling him up.

Arx ran up and used his horns to try and wrestle the fearblooms aside, but they bit at his head-frill, trying to drive him off. "Fight them, Gipsy!" He grabbed her hoof to stop her going under.

"You *must* fight them!"

But Gipsy
snatched her hoof
away – and conked herself
on the head with it. The fearblooms left
Teggs and Arx alone and crowded over
Gipsy.

With a final cry of "*Wiiiiiiiiiiiiiiibble!*"
the helpless hadrosaur disappeared into
the forest floor . . .

## Chapter Six

## GOING UNDERGROUND

"Gipsy!" Swinging his tail
like a pickaxe, Teggs
started digging at
the mud. "Hold
on, we'll get you
out!"

Arx pressed his head
against the disturbed
soil. "I can hear Gipsy!
She's still alive – and, er,
still wibbling."

"Those evil plants," muttered
Teggs, digging all the harder. "Attacking
her when she can't fight back – just like
they attacked Krokk."

61

"They might have attacked Frisbee, Yokul and the others too," Arx ventured. "We'd need to ask Leefer to be sure, but it sounds like Gipsy and Krokk were both acting as oddly as the farmers were before they vanished."

Teggs gasped. "Arx – you don't think the fearblooms are to blame for sending dinosaurs round the twist?"

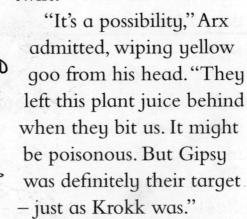

"It's a possibility," Arx admitted, wiping yellow goo from his head. "They left this plant juice behind when they bit us. It might be poisonous. But Gipsy was definitely their target – just as Krokk was."

Teggs wiped his own bruises on the grass. "I'm still weak from that carnivore booby-trap. Arx, help me dig. I'll call on all the dimorphodon for help." He threw back his head and whistled. "That should bring the whole flock flapping."

Arx nodded, burrowing with his horns "Hang in there, Gipsy – we're going to get you out!"

Back at the gigantosaurus rocket, Iggy was fiddling with the door controls. They were too high for him to reach on his own, so Sprite and some of the dimorphodon were flapping hard to support him in mid-air. A blue butterfly perched on his nose as if taking a rest. "Push off!" said Iggy, shooing it away. "Some of us are trying to work!"

Then Teggs's whistling call echoed urgently through the air. "That's the Captain!" Iggy realized.

"Eeep!" chirped Sprite in shocked reply. As one, the dimorphodon flock let go of Iggy and zoomed away.

"Whoa! *Oof!*" Iggy landed with a bump on his butt. "I wonder what Teggs needs them for?" He raised his communicator – but it wasn't working. "That blast of energy from the doors must have fried the circuits."

"Yes," came an icy whisper behind him. "It did."

Iggy jumped up, as a sour, chemical smell caught in his nostrils. "Who's there?"

64

"Why, the same cunning carnivore who captured your friend, of course." A grey gigantosaurus in a black skull-cap pushed out from the bushes, waving a jar full of mauve goo. "I am Gucklock the Poisoner. And unless you open that door at once, I shall destroy you with

this poisonous purple potion!"

"So it was *you* who tied up Gipsy." Iggy scowled at the soft-spoken carnivore. "We thought you were hiding inside your ship."

"That's what I wanted you to think," Gucklock gloated. "I used the female as bait to lure you here. I knew that once you'd discovered the rocket you would be determined to get inside . . . and that is exactly what *I* want. I can't afford any delays while you wait for your little flapping friends to come back and lift you high enough to work." Gucklock stomped towards him. "So, you can stand on my back instead."

Iggy held his nose and reluctantly clambered up the carnivore's thick neck. "You'll choke me to death first with your pong."

"That is merely the smell of my powerful poisons," Gucklock retorted. "If you can't open the door quickly, I'll show you exactly how powerful they are!"

"I already know," Iggy muttered.

"I've seen what you've done to the crops on this planet."

"Beautiful, isn't it? A whole planet – poisoned!" Gucklock sniggered. "We landed here two weeks ago under cover of a storm. We ran tests on the soil and the crops, and I experimented with different potions to see which would do the most damage. It didn't take long to create a germy spray that spreads super-swiftly through the air . . ."

Iggy's eyes narrowed as he tinkered with the controls. "Is that what turned Gipsy and the others funny?"

"No," Gucklock hissed. "What happened to your friend has happened to my crew too." He huffed a little forlornly. "I think I am the only one who has not been affected."

'Like Leefer – the only one of the farmers who's still normal," Iggy pondered.

"All twenty of my crewmates have

gone crazy now. Captain Krokk locked them away inside the ship. He hoped that with my knowledge of toxic science I could find a cure . . . But I could not. And then, Krokk went crazy too . . ."

"We noticed." Balanced precariously on the carnivore, Iggy reluctantly worked on. "What are you planning to do once you get inside?"

"Leave, of course, and get on with the mission!" said Gucklock. "There are still nine more of your filthy farm-worlds to poison before we can return home to Gigantos."

Iggy glared down at him. "If you destroy those crops, millions of plant-eaters will starve!"

"That's the whole idea," hissed Gucklock. "The Vegetarian Sector will be so weakened, it will quickly fall before the might of the Carnivore Space Force's invading armies." He chuckled.

"Once we have conquered, we can fatten the population back up again – ready to be eaten. Now, keep working."

"No!" said Iggy. "Do what you want with me – but I'll never help you!"

Gucklock roared with anger and threw back his head. Iggy lost his balance, and accidentally stuck his wrench into the heart of the controls. There was a shower of sparks and Iggy fell, striking the ground

with a thump that whumped the air from his lungs. Gucklock loomed over him . . .

But then, to Iggy's horror, the rocket's door hummed quietly open!

"Well, well. It seems you did help me, after all." Gucklock gave a throaty laugh and pulled a glass jar from his belt. "Many thanks, you leaf-chewing chump! Your reward is a gobful of this deadly poison. Mmm, tasty . . ."

"*Thanks, but he's already eaten!*" Without warning, Arx came charging out of the trees and rammed into the pongy poisoner, knocking him onto his side. The ground shook as the carnivore fell.

"Nice rescue, Arx!" Iggy beamed.

"You're not out of trouble yet," Arx reminded him.

Gucklock staggered back up, snarling. Arx bashed him in the belly with all three horns, and then Iggy sprang up and butted the monster under the chin. With a gargle of rage, Gucklock stumbled backwards into his ship and thwacked a button with his tail. The door slammed down with the force of a guillotine's blade.

"Fools," Gucklock rasped from behind the door. "Now I will take off and incinerate you – together with this entire forest!"

"He'll do it too," Iggy said worriedly. "What are you doing here, anyway? Why did you came back, where's Gipsy?"

"Your communicator's not working," Arx explained. "Gipsy's been dragged underground by fearblooms, and we need extra help getting her out."

"I wonder why she's been affected and the rest of us haven't?" Iggy frowned. "Mind you, underground might be the safest place to be if this rocket takes off . . ."

Suddenly the ground beneath their feet began to tremble and shake. The next moment, it collapsed completely! With a yell of alarm, both Iggy and Arx went tumbling into deep, soily darkness.

"OOF!" "ARGH!" They landed in a dazed heap. Flat on his back, Arx saw a round window of gloomy forest

high above – then heard the sound of
something heavy shuffling through the
darkness. Something coming closer . . .

## Chapter Seven

## TUNNEL VISIONS

Arx and Iggy held dead still as a sweet, sickly smell filled the freezing air ...

"I recognize that whiff!" Iggy cried, getting to his feet. "It's—"

"'Tunnel-explorer Leefer', they call me," came the lambeosaur's familiar voice. He put down his super-spade and switched on a torch. "Glad to see you! Where'd you drop in from?"

"The forest," Iggy informed him.

"Leefer's tunnel-digging must've weakened the ground beneath us," Arx realized.

"Not my tunnel," Leefer protested. "I was digging underneath the field when I fell through the ground too!"

"What happened then?" asked Iggy.

"Well, my super-spade got broken in the fall so I couldn't dig myself out again. I've been walking for miles through these tunnels, trying to find a way out. All the time we've been farming here, I had no idea they ever existed . . ." Leefer brightened, and handed Iggy a withered plant. "Still, at least I got that sample you wanted! Grabbed it just before I fell."

"Er, thank you," said Arx. "But we know now the crops have been poisoned by gigantosaurus invaders!"

Leefer's jaw dropped. "Truly?"

"They came here during that big storm a couple of weeks back and mixed up something horrible," Iggy informed him. "But whatever's sent your farmer friends funny has also affected the carnivores — *and* Gipsy."

"The fearblooms pulled her into
the mud along with Krokk the
gigantosaurus," Arx went on. "I suspect
they've dragged them down here."

Leefer gulped. "You mean . . . these
tunnels were made by the fearblooms?"

"I believe so," said Arx gravely, as
the sound of quiet scuttling edged into
their ears. "We've fallen right into the
fearblooms' lair!"

"Nonsense. I've not seen a single one
of them down here . . ." Leefer trained
his torch along the tunnel — to reveal
a bundle of the creepy plants, standing
mere metres away, swaying and snapping
their green jaws. "Until now, that is!"

"They must've heard us fall," said Arx, "and come looking."

"Time we weren't here," said Iggy.

"I think the fearblooms are thinking the same thing!" Arx said, as the looming plants rattled their roots and surged along the tunnel towards them. "Quick – run for it!"

The three dinosaurs sprinted away through the dark maze of tunnels. Arx led the

way, praying he didn't run straight into another plant ambush . . .

"I hate running," Leefer complained.

"Let me guess," puffed Iggy, racing

along beside him. "Hate-to-run Leefer, they call you."

"Exactly!" Leefer was astounded. "How did you know?"

After a couple of minutes, Arx stopped running and chanced a glance over his shoulder. There were no fearblooms in sight. "Let's rest for a moment," he said, and Iggy and Leefer flopped down gratefully. "I must try to get my bearings . . ."

Just then, Iggy jumped as something sprinkled over his nose. "Ugh! What's that?"

Leefer shone his torch at Iggy. "It's mud! Must be coming from . . ."

"Up there!" Iggy backed away as more dirt came crumbling down from the roof high above. "Look out – it's another cave-in!"

With a juddering rumble, the ceiling fell apart. Arx and Iggy dived aside and dragged Leefer with them as a ton of

rocky soil crashed down beside them
– along with a small, mucky, flapping
bundle and a grubby-looking orange-
brown stegosaurus ...

"Sprite! Captain Teggs!" Arx cried.
"Fancy bumping into you."

"More of a splat than a bump."
Iggy helped Teggs and Sprite to stand.
"Are you two all right?"

Sprite nodded and cheeped to the
other dimorphodon, warning them to
wait up above.

"We're fine, guys," said Teggs. "We were

just digging our way down to get to Gipsy when the ground gave way. How about you?"

Iggy and Arx quickly told their captain of their adventures – and watched his worried frown grow deeper and deeper.

"Somehow, we've got to rescue Gipsy and then get above ground to stop Gucklock," Teggs said. "How do the fearblooms come and go from down here to up there?"

"I think they use their vines, leaves and roots to climb up and down special shafts," said Arx. "Being plants, they can slip through the soil and hardly disturb it – even with a victim in tow."

"I guess we must've crashed through the top of one of those shafts," said Iggy.

"Do you suppose those filthy plants dragged my friends down here too?" asked Leefer.

"Shhh!" Arx hissed. "I just heard something."

Teggs froze. "Fearblooms?"

"Nope," came a croaky voice from behind them. "Farmers!"

Leefer shone his weedy torchbeam along the tunnel to reveal two more lambeosaurs in grubby checked shirts and dungarees. "Yokul! And Frisbee!" Leefer whooped and ran to greet them. "You're alive! You're not sick and crazy any more!"

"Look out, all of you," called Teggs, as a clutch of fearblooms came into sight. "Here come the creepy plant-creatures!" He reared up on his hind legs, ready to fight . . .

But Yokul ran over and held him back. "No! You don't understand."

"The fearblooms aren't our enemies," called Frisbee. "They saved us all from the big blue butterflies!"

81

Teggs, Arx and Iggy looked at each other, dumbfounded.

"I was wrong," said Leefer. "They *are* still crazy."

"We are not," Yokul insisted. He walked up to the fearblooms and stroked their leaves. The plants swayed happily. "See? They mean us no harm."

Arx frowned. "But we saw them biting our friend and dragging her down here."

"And they bit me and Arx when we tried to help her," Teggs added.

One of the fearblooms wriggled up to Iggy and chomped him on the nose.

"Ow! And now they've bitten *me*!" Iggy rubbed his hooter. "Ugh, I've got yellow slime all over my snout."

"It's not attacking you, my friend," said Frisbee calmly. "It is *healing* you."

Yokul nodded. "You've been touched by a butterfly, haven't you?"

"Er . . ." Iggy thought back. "Yeah, one landed on my nose for a second."

"A couple landed on me too," Teggs recalled.

"And me," said Arx.

"They didn't just land on you," said Frisbee. "They *stung* you without you noticing."

"I've studied the butterflies, you see," Yokul explained. "Though they look beautiful, they are very poisonous. And their sting is enough to drive a dinosaur demented. Victims start saying 'wibble', bump themselves on the bonce and run about in a daze. Eventually, if no treatment is given they grow wild and nasty." He sighed. "I'm afraid I became ill before I could warn my friends of the terrible truth. I've only just got better."

"Me too," said Frisbee.

"But where did these butterflies come from?" asked Teggs. "You were farming on Noxia-4 for years without any problem."

"Like the fearblooms, the butterflies were always here," Frisbee informed him. "But their venom was weak, it couldn't hurt a dinosaur."

"The fearblooms fed on the butterflies, then as now," said Yokul.

"Then something changed. The butterflies quickly grew more and more poisonous."

"We know one thing that changed," said Leefer. "Sneaky carnivores landed here and killed our crops."

Frisbee gasped. "Then someone *did* come here from space to poison the land. I was right!"

"But you were wrong to think that some robots could stop them," said Iggy, rubbing his bruises. "These poisoners were hiding out in the forest the whole time."

"And not just hiding," breathed Arx. "Gucklock said that he and his crew brewed up all sorts of vile poisonous mixtures while making their germ-spray. They must have dumped loads of toxic waste – polluting the forest around them. And I'll bet the butterflies absorbed that pollution. Somehow, it made them change ..."

Teggs nodded grimly. "It turned them from harmless insects into killers!"

"Looks like you were right all along, Leefer," Iggy murmured. "It really is a forest of evil – and the meat-brain who made it that way is all set to get away scot free!"

## Chapter Eight

## FEAR-BOOM!

"Somehow, we've got to put things right and make this planet well again," said Teggs. "Yokul, that yellow stuff a fearbloom leaves behind when it chomps someone – are you saying it actually cures the butterflies' victims?"

Yokul nodded. "It seems that fearblooms are very tough – they are not affected by poison or pollution. They eat the butterflies with no ill effects and pass on their immunity through their spit – which is quickly absorbed by the skin."

"It stops the infection and calms the victim," Frisbee went on. "But recovery time depends on the victim's physical fitness and how many stings they received."

Arx nodded thoughtfully. "We were bitten soon after we were stung, and so we were cured before we noticed a thing. I suppose Gipsy wasn't so lucky."

"That's right," said Yokul. "The fearblooms take the sickest dinosaurs underground to keep them safe while they get better. Let me show you."

Frisbee led the way along another tunnel. Teggs, Iggy, Arx and Leefer followed, trailed by Yokul and the fearblooms.

"How come I wasn't bitten?" Leefer wondered.

"Perhaps the butterflies don't like strong smells," mused Iggy. "That would explain why they left Gucklock alone too."

Leefer frowned. "Are you saying I smell?"

"You do smell," said Frisbee bluntly.
"'Too-much-aftershave Leefer', we call
you."

"Oh." Leefer sniffed his armpits and
nodded. "Fair enough."

The passage widened into a muddy
cavern, where three sleeping dinosaurs in
dungarees lay on beds of leaves.

"Our friends were stung very badly,"
said Yokul, "so it's taking them longer to
get better."

But Teggs pushed past
them. He'd spotted a
familiar stripy shape
in an adjoining
cave ... "Gipsy!" He
grinned with delight
and knelt beside
her bed. "Are you all
right?"

"Hello, Captain. I'm
sorry for dozing off ..." Gipsy yawned
and stretched – and winced. "Ow! What
happened? I'm sore all over ..."

"The pain will soon pass," Frisbee
assured her. "Butterflies stung you."

"But the fearblooms have made you
well again," Arx told her happily.

"And look!" Iggy had found yet
another side-cave – one that reeked of
old meat. "They're even healing laughing
boy here."

Frisbee, Yokul and Leefer came over
to see – then quickly ran away again.

"Aaaagh!" yelped Yokul. "A meat-eater!"

"Meet Captain Krokk," said Iggy, "the carnivore crumb who led the mission to spoil this world."

Teggs glared at the curled-up carnivore. "Well, Gucklock might blast off from here with his sick crewmates, but at least his boss is our prisoner."

"Wait!" Captain Krokk struggled up, looking cross-eyed. He was still plainly unwell. "Did you say . . . Gucklock is planning to blast off?"

"He's dead set on it," said Iggy.

"Dead is right." Feebly, Krokk slumped back onto his leafy bed. "The Carnivore Space Force cannot allow top secret

Solar-Storm technology to fall into enemy hands – so when I left the ship I set the burglar alarm." He glared up at Teggs. "If anyone besides me tries to take off in that ship, it will blow up with the force of an exploding star."

Leefer almost fainted, and Gipsy's headcrest glowed so blue with alarm it brightened the cave. "We'll all be killed!" she cried.

"Even if we could reach our shuttle in time," said Iggy, "we could never fit everyone inside."

"The blast will blow Noxia-4 apart," Arx murmured. "And then the planet's rocky remains will bombard the other farm planets in this sector – leaving them devastated."

Frisbee gulped. "Millions of plant-eaters will starve!"

"Krokk, how do we turn off the alarm?" Teggs demanded.

"I . . . I can't remember," said Krokk weakly.

"He's still in a daze," Yokul noted. "He must've been stung a lot."

"I wouldn't tell you even if I knew," Krokk rasped. "I'd rather die than become your prisoner!"

"Don't be a fool!" Teggs shouted. "Think. You *must* remember!"

But Krokk was already asleep once more.

"What are we going to do?" said Gipsy.

"That warship hasn't gone boom yet," said Teggs. "We've still got a chance to switch off that burglar alarm."

"But how are we going to reach the surface in time?" asked Frisbee.

Leefer nodded. "I've broken my superspade."

"And we'll never dig our own way up in time," said Iggy.

"The dimorphodon will help us," Teggs declared. "They can air-lift us out through the hole we made through the tunnel roof."

Sprite nodded bravely – then some fearblooms shuffled forward. They quickly coiled their steely stalks around Iggy and raised him into the air. "Hey!" he protested. "What's going on?"

"The fearblooms will help us as well!" Arx grinned. "They can drag dinosaurs down through the mud, and they can lift them up through it too!"

"Brilliant!" Gipsy stroked one of the fearbloom's leaves and it nuzzled her. "They really are kindly plants."

"And they'll die with the rest of us if that warship explodes," said Teggs. "Plants and plant-eaters, we must all fight together – in a battle to the end!"

Within minutes, the astrosaurs and their unusual allies were back breathing fresh air in the forest. The fearblooms had hauled Teggs, Arx, Frisbee and Yokul through the mud and mulch, while the dimorphodon dangled Iggy, Gipsy and Leefer from their beaks and claws. Everyone kept a sharp eye out for butterflies.

"There's not a moment to lose," said Teggs, wriggling free of a fearbloom. "Is everyone ready?"

The others nodded grimly, and Leefer wielded his bent super-spade like a club. "'Born-ready Leefer', they call me," he said.

"Then – CHARGE!" yelled Teggs. Whirling his tail over his head like a spiky battle-axe he charged off along the well-trampled path back to the warship. Arx and the farmers ran along behind, while Iggy helped

Gipsy keep up at the rear. Sprite and his full flight-crew flapped gamely overhead, and the fearblooms fanned out through the undergrowth like leafy shadows – all converging on the gigantosaurus ship.

"There it is!" Teggs cried, bursting through the bracken that ringed the rocket's gloomy clearing. "Iggy, can you open it safely?"

"Safely?" Gipsy echoed. "With Gucklock the poisoner on board with his horrible crewmates?"

"I'll have a go." Iggy pulled out his astro-wrench – and the door slid open!

"Wow, you're good," said Leefer, impressed.

But then a gigantosaurus came
pounding outside in a panic. It was
Gucklock. He saw the crowd gathered
around the ship and bared his teeth – but
Teggs tripped him with a tail-swipe.

KER-*THOMP*! Gucklock turned a
somersault and landed flat on his face.

Gipsy jumped on the carnivore's back,
pinning him to the ground. "Going
somewhere, Gucklock?"

"Yes – to steal your shuttle and escape,"

wheezed Gucklock. "I tried to leave in my own ship, but set off the burglar alarm. Now the Solar-Storm engines are going to self-destruct!"

"Just as Krokk said," Iggy groaned. "Then we're too late!"

Already, Teggs could feel a low, subsonic rumble building in the rocket beside them. "How long now before that ship explodes?"

"Not more than five minutes." Gucklock struggled to get away. "Let me go! Let me go right now, or you'll be sorry."

"Oh yes, poisoner?" Frisbee sneered. "And why's that?"

Gucklock glared up at him. "Because when I was trying to turn off the burglar alarm, I accidentally turned loose

my loopy crewmates. They're running wild, out for blood – and chasing after me."

Yokul looked pale. "They'll be in the final, nastiest stages of butterfly poisoning."

Leefer almost dropped his spade in terror. "They'll eat us alive!"

Sure enough, over the rising thrum of the doomed ship's defence system, Teggs could hear the clatter and stomp of footsteps rushing towards them. "Look out, everyone," he cried. "Here they come!"

## Chapter Nine

## KILLER COUNTDOWN

Chaos broke out in the clearing!

Hordes of snarling gigantosaurus
stormed outside and roared at their prey.
The biggest of them loomed over Teggs.

"You have to let us pass!" Teggs cried.
"If you don't, we're all doomed!"

But the carnivore only bellowed
"WIBBLE!" and slashed at

him with killer claws. Teggs
blocked the blow with his backplates
and swung his tail, clubbing his attacker
into a tree. A flock of dimorphodon
descended at once, battering the beast
with their wings and claws.

That same moment, Iggy came under
attack. A gigantosaurus knocked him to
the ground and flung itself at him – but
Iggy rolled aside and the monster's jaws
closed on nothing but mud.

Arx made sure to trample the brute
on his way to save Yokul and Frisbee
from two more. He charged into the

gigantosaurus, shoving them
into nearby bushes.

The rocket's rumbling was getting
louder now, and smoke was starting to
curl from its casing. "We've got to get
inside," Teggs cried.

"Easier said than done – I'm still
feeling a bit dizzy!" Gipsy rolled off
Gucklock as another gigantosaurus
bounded out from the warship, stomping
on the poisoner's head as it came to get
her. But Sprite came shooting to her aid
with a half-dozen dimorphodon. They
dive-bombed the meat-muncher, pecking

and scratching. Roaring and wibbling with anger, the gigantosaurus sank to its knees – and Leefer whacked it round the head with his broken super-spade.

"Yahoo!" he cheered as it flopped to the forest floor. "Fighting-champ Leefer, they call me!"

Two fearblooms pushed past Teggs and grabbed hold of his

gigantosaurus foe, chomping hard and precisely, trying to heal its madness. More and more of

the plants were flocking to the glade. As
fast as the astrosaurs and their friends
could knock Krokk's crew to the ground,
the fearblooms seized them with stems,
leaves and jaws, biting them better.

Gipsy used a tree branch to beat
back the last wild carnivore – then
Frisbee took it from her. "Go on inside,
astrosaurs," he cried. "The dimorphodon
and the fearblooms will help us take
charge of these dung-heads – while you
stop the ship from self-destructing!"

Yokul nodded. "Go
on, before it's too
late."

Teggs nodded,
snagged Gucklock's
belt with a tail spike
and pulled him to
his feet. "Wakey-
wakey. We need you
to take us to your
control room."

"It's too late," Gucklock gasped as
smoke poured from the warship's sides.
"The miniature sun inside will erupt at
any moment."

"But it hasn't yet," Arx pointed out.
"There's still hope."

Teggs shoved Gucklock into the
shaking ship. "So, get going!"

The astrosaurs marched after him
through the dark, smelly corridors
of the top-secret warship. It was
jungle-hot, and a scary sizzling sound
was coming from the walls. Teggs felt
faint explosions going off deep inside
the ship, each one a little louder and
harder than the last. *We must be in time*

*to stop it exploding,* he told himself fiercely. *We must!*

At last they reached the control room – a vast, circular space, bathed in fierce red light. Posts and pillars coated with knobs and levers stuck out from the floor and walls, and a screen on the wall was counting down large crimson numbers: *79 . . . 78 . . . 77 . . .*

"Quickly!" Teggs grabbed hold of Gucklock. "Where are the controls for the burglar alarm?"

Gucklock picked up a mangled scarlet lever from the floor, trailing wires. "Er . . . some of it's here." He shrugged and pointed to a hole in one of the posts. "When the alarm started I tried to turn it off again . . ."

Arx groaned. "You tried a bit too hard!"

Iggy reached into the hole in the post with his astro-wrench. "It's no good," he said. "I can't reach the workings."

Gipsy's blue head–crest seemed purple in the red lights. "If only we had weapons we could try blasting it."

"I tried that," said Gucklock. "I've tried everything."

The rocket shook harder. The ceiling was smoking.

Teggs looked up at the screen.

*61 ... 60 ... 59 ...*

"Not fair!" Gucklock stamped a big, scaly foot against the steaming metal floor. "I am Gucklock, the master poisoner! I cannot die a prisoner of plant-eaters ..." He grabbed a flask of white powder from this belt. "My final act will be to poison you all!"

Gipsy whopped his wrist with a dino-judo chop and caught the flask as he dropped it. "*My final act will be to sock your lights out!*" she snarled. "This is all your fault!"

"Wait, Gipsy!" Teggs snatched the flask from her. "Poison – maybe that's the answer!"

Iggy looked blank. "The answer to what?"

Teggs grabbed more jars and tubs and capsules from Gucklock's belt. "You can poison a planet – what about a computer?"

Gucklock stared at them. "Poison a machine? You're out of your minds!"

"We're almost out of time!" Gipsy hooted. *39 . . . 38 . . . 37 . . .*

"Well, if Gucklock won't even try, I will!" Arx grabbed the glass containers and lined them up on the floor. "Let me see . . . sonk drops and bertle-berry juice, tankpox and rash-bobbles . . ."

"Hurry, Arx," Iggy urged him. "There's just 29 seconds left!"

"If we mix them all together it should make a sort of acid," said Arx. "Strong enough to melt wires and circuits."

"Or it might blow us all to bits!" said Gucklock.

Another *BANG* rang through the rippling walls of the doomed rocket.

"What does it matter now?" asked Teggs grimly. "Let's do it!"

## Chapter Ten

## POTION POWER

The lights were flickering. The heat was rising. Carefully, Teggs opened the jar of rash-bobbles. Arx added a few drops of bertle-berry juice and Gipsy poured in the tankpox and sonk drops.

Iggy stirred the mixture with the tip of his astro-wrench, which suddenly started to melt. "I think this stuff's ready!" he shouted.

Gucklock sank to his knees. "Twenty seconds to go!" The whole rocket was rocking from side to side.

Teggs ran to the hole in the controls and poured in the poisonous concoction.

111

Thick, black smoke rushed out from inside. He fell back reeling and choking. The smoke eclipsed the numbers on the screen . . .

But when it cleared, the numbers were still counting down! *13 . . . 12 . . . 11 . . .*

"The acid didn't work!" Gipsy wailed.

Arx shook his head sadly. "I'm afraid the mixture wasn't quite toxic enough."

Then Teggs sniffed and frowned. "Ugh! What's that smell?"

"Um . . . it's me." Gucklock blushed red. "I'm so scared, I just pooped myself."

"Well, thanks a lot!" Iggy held his

snout. "Just what I want to sniff in my last moments."

"Perhaps it *is*!" Teggs bounded over to the heap of slimy droppings. "You wanted toxic, Arx – it doesn't get much nastier than Gucklock's grotty gift here. I wonder . . ."

Gipsy's gaze was gripped by the countdown on the screen. "Five seconds left!" she squealed.

Gritting his teeth, Teggs socked the pile of muck with his tail. It flew through the air . . .

"Four . . ." yelled Gipsy.

A big, sludgy splat burst over the controls.

"Three . . ."

"Cross your fingers!" Teggs yelled over the smouldering roar of the rising solar-storm. "Cross your tails, legs and anything else!"

"Two . . . !"

The astrosaurs clung together, eyes shut tight, braced for the final blistering bang . . .

But it never came. Instead, the ship
stopped shaking, and the ominous
rumbling began to die away.

Teggs opened his eyes to find the
lights had changed from danger-
red to welcoming white. Already the
temperature was starting to drop.

"It worked!" Teggs breathed. "That
toxic gunk took out the burglar alarm!"

"Gucklock started this mess," said Arx,
"and now his mess has finally stopped
it!"

"So – goodbye, fools!"
Gucklock turned to
run. "No one makes
a prisoner of me-ee
– *agghh*!" He slipped
on his own dung
and conked his
head on a control
post – then flopped
in a daze back to
the messy floor.

"Ha!" said Iggy. "Back in the poo where he belongs!"

Teggs took hold of the dozing dinosaur's tail. "Come on," he told his friends. "We'll take him outside and check on the others. I hope they're all right!"

When the astrosaurs emerged from the warship carrying Gucklock between them, they saw that the answer was a definite YES. The forest floor was littered with gigantosaurus, all pinned to the ground by fearblooms and dimorphodon. Frisbee and Yokul were leaning on each other, scuffed and sweaty from their battle – while Leefer was performing a strange victory dance with another of the plants, swinging it round by the leaves while shaking his bottom.

"'Disco-sensation Leefer', they call me!" he panted proudly. "When they're not calling me 'Carnivore-kicker Leefer' or 'Punch-a-gigantosaurus Leefer' or—"

"Well done, Leefer!" Teggs grinned.

"Astrosaurs!" Frisbee and Yokul rushed over excitedly. "The rocket's stopped rocking! You did it!"

"With a little help from Gucklock, here," Iggy agreed.

"But while the planet's safe, our entire harvest is still ruined," said Frisbee.

Gipsy placed a hoof on his shoulder. "At least we caught the dinos who did it — and your farmer friends will soon be well again."

Yokul nodded. "That's wonderful, of course — but it won't feed those starving dinosaurs."

"True," agreed Arx with a smile. "But I wouldn't give up on your harvest just yet. We might just be able to save it – with help from the fearblooms."

Leefer looked at him oddly. "Huh?"

"The fearblooms can resist poisons and pollution, and their sap heals infections – right?" Arx approached one of the plants and held out his arm; the fearbloom chomped it politely, leaving a smear of yellow. "Perhaps it will heal the crops too?"

Teggs whistled, impressed. "Sounds like a theory that needs putting to the test!"

"Quick, Leefer," said Iggy. "Have you still got that crop sample?"

"Sure do." Leefer reached into his dungarees, produced the battered,

wizened plant he'd managed to pluck
from the mud and tossed it over.

"OK, here goes . . ." Arx took the
measly crop and dipped it in the

fearbloom sap. Within
moments, the
shrivelled leaves
grew fatter and
greener. "There!
It will need
to be mixed
with other
ingredients to
make a proper
antidote, but . . ."

"It's a miracle," Frisbee declared,
carefully cradling the puffed-up plant.
"Noxia-4's harvest will be saved!"

"Yahooooo!" Leefer started dancing
with the fearbloom once more, and Yokul
joined in.

"Arx, you've proved it again," said
Gipsy, kissing the triceratops fondly on

the cheek. "You're the brightest spark in space."

"He certainly is!" Iggy smiled. "And I'll prove I'm the best mechanic in space – by building a special, super-sized sprinkler underneath the *Sauropod*. Then when Arx has cooked up enough of that antidote stuff . . ."

"We can fly around the planet and spray the fields." Teggs beamed. "That'll bring the crops back to life. When Krokk, Gucklock and all the others are fit again, we'll take them straight to space prison."

"And let DSS experts dismantle that warship safely," Arx added.

"Looks like everything's coming up roses," said Teggs happily. "And while I'm certainly no farmer, my crew is the cream of the crop – and my hopes of starting a new adventure soon are *growing* all the time!"

As the astrosaurs danced about with

the farmers, celebrating their great
victory, they couldn't know that they
were indeed poised on the brink of
another adventure.

Perhaps the greatest and most
incredible adventure of all . . .

Visit www.**stevecolebooks**.co.uk for fun, games, jokes, to meet the characters and much, much more!

Welcome to a world where dinosaurs fly spaceships and cows use a time-machine . . .

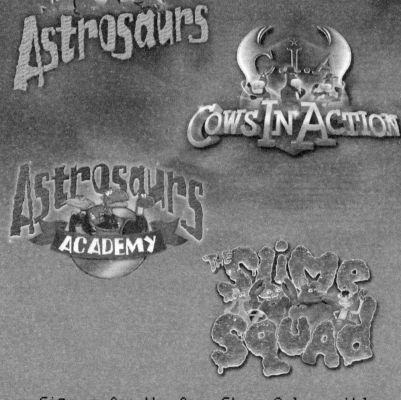

Sign up for the free Steve Cole monthly newsletter to find out what your favourite author is up to!

# ASTRO PUZZLE TIME

## THE PLANET OF PERIL
### QUIZ Questions

1. Where did the bonkers farmers send their distress call?
2. What was the name of the planet they farmed?
3. Which gigantosaurus was leader of the Carnivore Space Force Sneaky Missions Squad?
4. What kind of spaceship was owned by the carnivores?
5. Why did the butterflies not attack Leefer?
6. What toxic substance did the astrosaurs use to stop the rocket self-destructing?

## Answers:

1. A greengrocer's on the planet Steggos
2. Noxia-4
3. Captain Krokk
4. A Solar-storm warship
5. They didn't like the smell of his aftershave
6. Bucklock's slimy droppings

# ASTRO PUZZLE TIME

A space computer-virus has infected the *Sauropod*'s data-banks and scrambled the names of the astrosaurs! Solve the anagrams and match them to the correct crew-members.

THE SCRAMBLED NAMES:

1. Suggest ego star
2. Sir guinea spy
3. An ox roar
4. Hidden hop motor
5. Tight go yo

THE CREW:

Gipsy Saurine ✷
Iggy Tooth
Arx Orano
Teggs Stegosaur
The dimorphodon

Now take each of the correctly-spelled words and fit them into the grid below. The letters in the bigger boxes spell out the name of the astrosaurs' next destination . . .

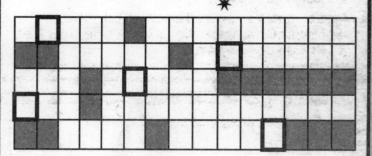

## ANSWERS:

✷ And the secret destination for the Astrosaurs next mission is _ _ _ _ _

The astrosaurs will return for their
amazing 20th full-length mission in

# Earth Attack!

Teggs's arch-enemy, General Loki, has
stolen a time machine. The astrosaurs
trail him to Earth in the distant past,
before the dinosaurs took off into space.
Soon they uncover a terrifying plot to
murder millions and destroy history . . .
but can they stop it?

# ALSO BY STEVE COLE

# IF YOU CAN'T TAKE THE SLIME
# DON'T DO THE CRIME!

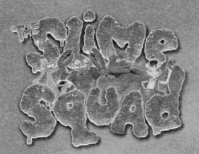

Plog, Furp, Zill and Danjo aren't just
monsters in a rubbish dump. They are
crime-busting super-monsters,
here to save their whiffy world!